My LiTTLE PONY

When Cutie Calls

D0951112

Special thanks to Erin Comella, Robert Fewkes, Heather Hopkins, Valerie Jurries, Ed Lane, Brian Lenard, Marissa Mansolillo, Donna Tobin, Michael Vogel, Mark Wiesenhahn, and Michael Kelly for their invaluable assistance.

ISBN: 978-1-61377-830-2
18 17 16 15     4 5 6 7
www.**IDWPUBLISHING**.com

**IDW**

Licensed By:
Hasbro

Ted Adams, CEO & Publisher
Greg Goldstein, President & COO
Robbie Robbins, EVP/Sr. Graphic Artist
Chris Ryall, Chief Creative Officer/Editor-in-Chief
Matthew Ruzicka, CPA, Chief Financial Officer
Alan Payne, VP of Sales
Dirk Wood, VP of Marketing
Lorelei Bunjes, VP of Digital Services

# When Cutie Calls

**Call of the Cutie**
Written by
**Megan McCarthy**

**The Cutie Mark Chronicles**
Written by
**Mitch Larson**

Adaptation by
**Justin Eisinger**

Edits by
**Alonzo Simon**

Lettering and Design by
**Tom B. Long**

# MEET THE PONIES

## Twilight Sparkle

TWILIGHT SPARKLE TRIES TO FIND THE ANSWER TO EVERY QUESTION! WHETHER STUDYING A BOOK OR SPENDING TIME WITH PONY FRIENDS, SHE ALWAYS LEARNS SOMETHING NEW!

## Spike

SPIKE IS TWILIGHT SPARKLE'S BEST FRIEND AND NUMBER ONE ASSISTANT. HIS FIRE BREATH CAN DELIVER SCROLLS DIRECTLY TO PRINCESS CELESTIA!

## Applejack

APPLEJACK IS HONEST, FRIENDLY, AND SWEET TO THE CORE! SHE LOVES TO BE OUTSIDE, AND HER PONY FRIENDS KNOW THEY CAN ALWAYS COUNT ON HER.

# Fluttershy

FLUTTERSHY IS A KIND AND GENTLE PONY WITH A BIG HEART. SHE LIKES TO TAKE CARE OF OTHERS, ESPECIALLY HER LITTLE ANIMAL FRIENDS.

# Rarity

RARITY KNOWS HOW TO ADD SPARKLE TO ANY OUTFIT! SHE LOVES TO GIVE HER PONY FRIENDS ADVICE ON THE LATEST PONY FASHIONS AND HAIRSTYLES.

# Pinkie Pie

PINKIE PIE KEEPS HER
PONY FRIENDS LAUGHING
AND SMILING ALL DAY!
CHEERFUL AND PLAYFUL,
SHE ALWAYS LOOKS ON
THE BRIGHT SIDE.

# Rainbow Dash

RAINBOW DASH LOVES TO
FLY AS FAST AS SHE CAN!
SHE IS ALWAYS READY TO
PLAY A GAME, GO ON AN
ADVENTURE, OR HELP OUT
ONE OF HER PONY FRIENDS.

# Princess Celestia

PRINCESS CELESTIA IS
A MAGICAL AND BEAUTIFUL
PONY WHO RULES THE LAND
OF ESQUESTRIA. ALL OF
THE PONIES IN PONYVILLE
LOOK UP TO HER!

CALL
OF THE
CUTIE

DING DONG

LET'S QUIET DOWN, PLEASE.

"WE HAVE A VERY IMPORTANT LESSON TO GET TO."

THANK YOU.

TODAY WE ARE GOING TO BE TALKING ABOUT CUTIE MARKS.

BOR-ING.

YOU CAN ALL SEE *MY* CUTIE MARK, CAN'T YOU?

LIKE ALL PONIES, I WASN'T BORN WITH A CUTIE MARK.

MY *FLANK* WAS *BLANK.*

THEN ONE DAY, WHEN I WAS ABOUT YOUR AGE...

...I WOKE UP TO FIND THAT A CUTIE MARK HAD APPEARED.

LOOK AT HER *HAIR*.

HE HE HE HE

YES, I KNOW, BUT HONESTLY, THAT'S HOW EVERYPONY WAS WEARING THEIR MANE BACK THEN.

I HAD DECIDED TO BECOME A TEACHER...

...AND THE FLOWERS SYMBOLIZED MY HOPE THAT I COULD HELP MY FUTURE STUDENTS *BLOOM* IF I NURTURED THEM WITH KNOWLEDGE.

THE SMILES REPRESENTED THE *CHEER* I HOPED TO BRING TO MY LITTLE PONIES WHILE THEY WERE LEARNING.

NOW, CAN ANYONE TELL ME WHEN A PONY GETS HIS OR HER CUTIE MARK?

OH! OH! OH! WHEN *STHE DISCOVERTHS* THAT *THERTAIN STHOMETHIN'* THAT *MAKESTH* HER *STHPETHIAL.*

THAT'S RIGHT, TWIST. A CUTIE MARK APPEARS ON A PONY'S FLANK WHEN HE OR SHE FINDS THAT CERTAIN SOMETHING THAT MAKES THEM DIFFERENT FROM EVERY OTHER PONY.

DISCOVERING WHAT MAKES YOU UNIQUE ISN'T SOMETHING...

...THAT HAPPENS OVERNIGHT. AND NO AMOUNT OF HOPING, WISHING...

PSST

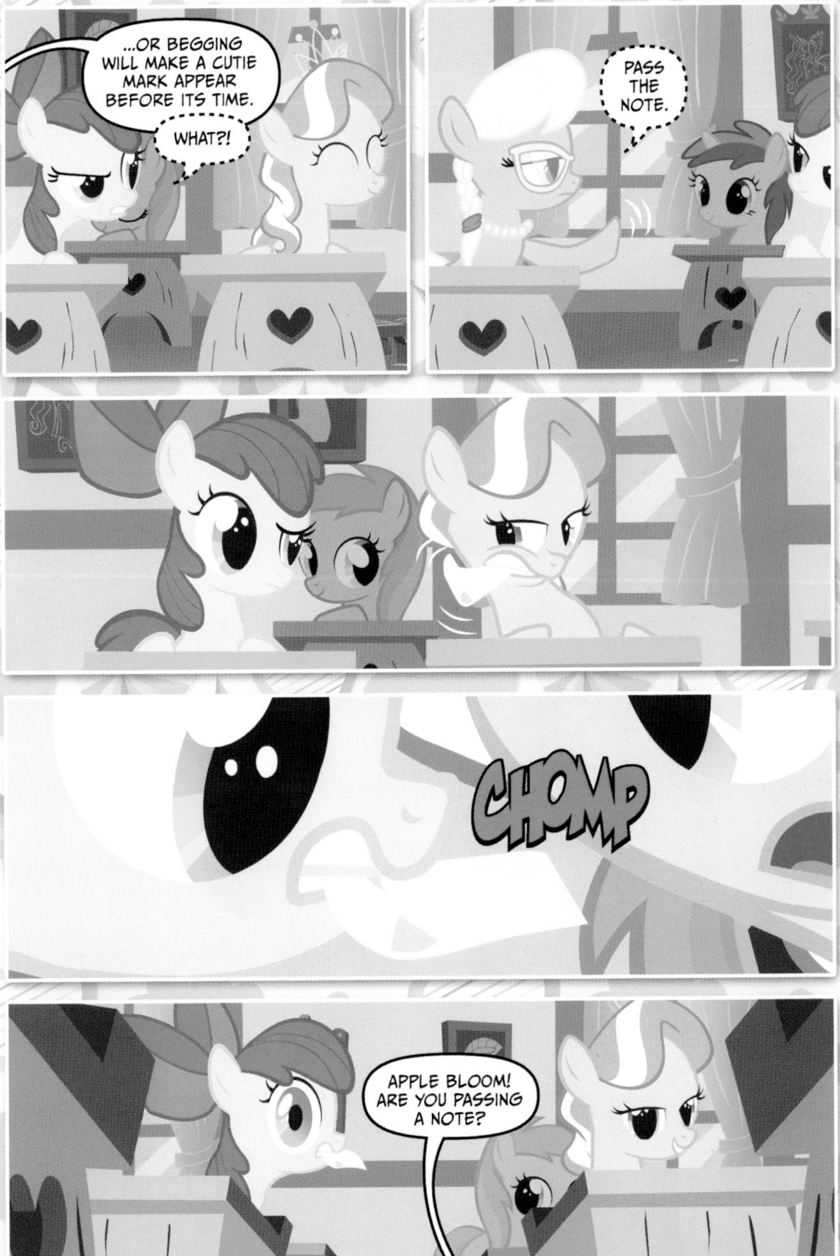

...OR BEGGING WILL MAKE A CUTIE MARK APPEAR BEFORE ITS TIME.
WHAT?!
PASS THE NOTE.
CHOMP
APPLE BLOOM! ARE YOU PASSING A NOTE?

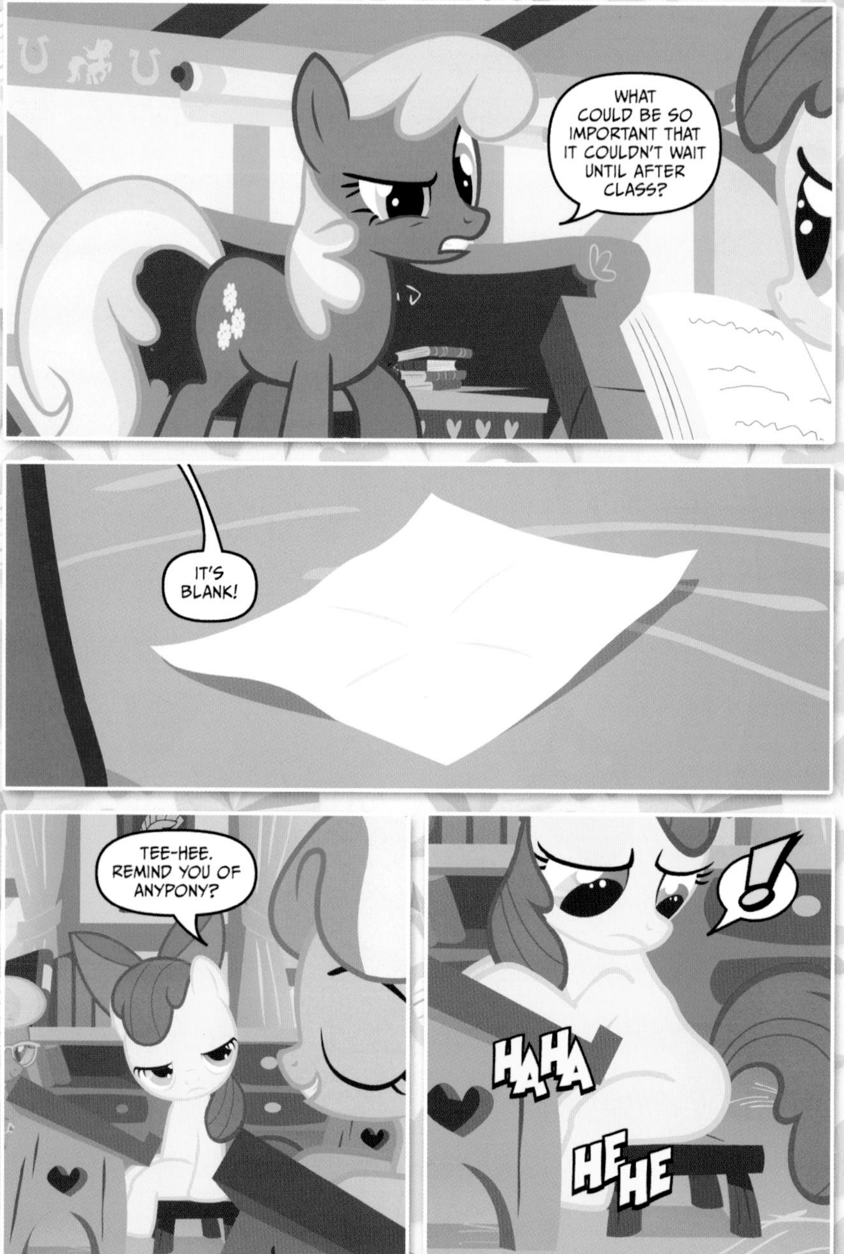
WHAT COULD BE SO IMPORTANT THAT IT COULDN'T WAIT UNTIL AFTER CLASS?
IT'S BLANK!
TEE-HEE. REMIND YOU OF ANYPONY?
!
HAHA
HEHE

DING DONG

CLOP CLOP CLOP

WANT *THOMETHING THWEET?* I'VE GOT *THOME* PEPPERMINT STICKTHS...

UH-UH.

THEY'LL MAKE YOU *THMILE.*

I MADE THEM *MYTHELF...*

I DON'T KNOW WHY WE HAD TO SIT THROUGH A LECTURE ABOUT GETTING A CUTIE MARK.

I MEAN, WAITING FOR YOUR CUTIE MARK IS SOOO LAST WEEK.

YOU'VE GOT YOURS...

...I JUST GOT MINE.

WE *ALL* HAVE THEM ALREADY.

I MEAN, *ALMOST* ALL OF US HAVE THEM ALREADY.

DON'T WORRY YOU TWO, YOU'RE STILL TOTALLY INVITED TO MY CUTE-CINERA THIS WEEKEND.

IT'S GOING TO BE AMAZING.

IT'S A PARTY CELEBRATING ME AND MY FANTASTIC CUTIE MARK. HOW COULD IT NOT BE?

GIMME A BREAK.

SEE YOU THIS WEEKEND...

...BLANK FLANKS!

HE HE HE HE

HE HE HE HE

LATER THAT DAY, AT SWEET APPLE ACRES...

IT'S NOT FAIR.

IT'S JUST NOT FAIR!

DON'T GET YOUR MANE IN A TANGLE. YOU'LL GET YOUR CUTIE MARK.

EVERYPONY GETS ONE EVENTUALLY.

BUT I DON'T WANT ONE *EVENTUALLY.* I WANT ONE **RIGHT NOOOOOOOW.**

I CAN'T GO TO DIAMOND TIARA'S CUTE-CINERA WITHOUT ONE. I JUST CAN'T.

COURSE YOU CAN.

YOU KNOW, I WAS THE LAST PONY IN MY CLASS TO GET A CUTIE MARK.

AND I COULDN'T BE PROUDER OF IT.

I KNEW MY FUTURE WAS TO RUN SWEET APPLE ACRES AND THESE BRIGHT SHINY APPLES SEALED THE DEAL!

COME TO THINK OF IT, GRANNY SMITH WAS THE LAST ONE IN HER CLASS TOO. SAME WITH BIG MCINTOSH.

I REALLY DON'T SEE HOW *THAT'S* SUPPOSED TO MAKE ME FEEL BETTER.

IT PROBABLY MEANS BEING THE LAST ONE IN YOUR CLASS TO GET A CUTIE MARK RUNS IN THE FAMILY.

...RUNS IN THE FAMILY...?

RUNS IN THE FAMILY!

YOU'VE GOT APPLES FOR YOUR CUTIE MARK!

GRANNY SMITH HAS AN APPLE PIE!

BIG MCINCTOSH HAS AN APPLE HALF!

MY UNIQUE TALENT MUST HAVE SOMETHING TO DO WITH APPLES!

APPLE BLOOM DECIDES TO HELP APPLEJACK AT THE MARKET.

GET YOUR DELICIOUS, NUTRITIOUS APPLES HERE.

DELICIOUS *AND* NUTRITIOUS. AND SO MANY USES!

CHOMP

YOU CAN EAT THEM!

"PLAY WITH THEM."

WHAMP

SPLURT

CREATE FINE ART FOR YOUR HOME WITH THEM...

...YOU'D HAVE TO BE CRAZY NOT TO GET A BUSHEL OF YOUR VERY OWN.

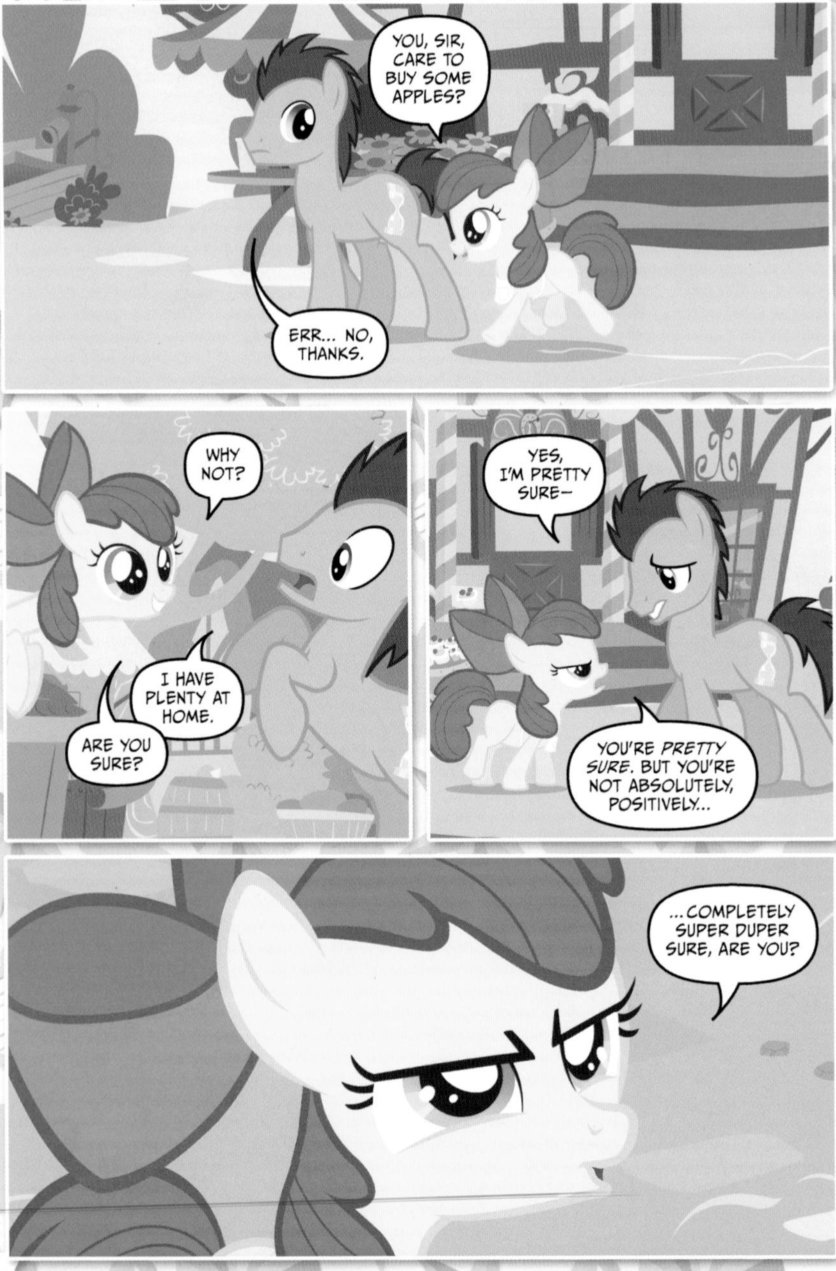
YOU, SIR, CARE TO BUY SOME APPLES?
ERR... NO, THANKS.
WHY NOT?
I HAVE PLENTY AT HOME.
ARE YOU SURE?
YES, I'M PRETTY SURE–
YOU'RE *PRETTY SURE*. BUT YOU'RE NOT ABSOLUTELY, POSITIVELY...
...COMPLETELY SUPER DUPER SURE, ARE YOU?

IF I BUY SOME APPLES WILL YOU PLEASE LEAVE ME ALONE?

AL-RIGHT!

WOO-HOO! THAT IS HOW YOU SELL SOME APPLES AND GET A CUTIE MARK!

SO, WHAT DOES MY CUTIE MARK LOOK LIKE?

A SHOPPING BAG FULL OF APPLES? A SATISFIED CUSTOMER EATING AN APPLE?

HMMM. MAYBE I GOTTA INCREASE MY SALES FIGURES FIRST.

SORRY, LITTLE SIS, BUT YOUR APPLE SELLING DAYS ARE OVER.

WHAT?! BUT HOW ELSE AM I GONNA GET MY CUTIE MARK?

HOME. NOW.

〈HMPF〉

LISTEN, SUGARCUBE. I KNOW IT'S HARD TO WAIT FOR YOUR VERY OWN CUTIE MARK, BUT YOU JUST CAN'T FORCE IT.

BESIDES, YOU'RE NOT THAT GROWN UP JUST YET.

AIN'T THERE OTHER FILLIES IN YOUR CLASS WITHOUT ONE?

WELL.... TWIST DOESN'T HAVE HERS YET.

DO YA THINK YOU'D FEEL BETTER IF YOU WENT TO THE PARTY WITH HER?

MM-HMM.

WELL THERE YA GO!

BET YOU AND TWIST WOULD HAVE A GREAT TIME TOGETHER. NOW RUN ALONG AND FIND YOUR FRIEND.

YOU'RE SURE YOU DON'T WANT ME TO STICK AROUND UNTIL THE END OF THE MARKET?

HEY! WHO'S BEEN USING MY RACKET?!

YEP. I'M SURE.

KNOCK KNOCK

OH. *WHAT'TH* UP, APPLE BLOOM?

SO I WAS THINKING... MAYBE WE COULD GO TO DIAMOND TIARA'S CUTE-CINERA TOGETHER.

I DON'T HAVE A CUTIE MARK... YOU DON'T HAVE A CUTIE MARK.

WELL, UM...

ITHN'T MY CUTIE MARK THWELL?

GAW—

I'VE ALWAYTH LOVED MAKING MY OWN STHAVORY STHWEETH...

...BUT IT TOOK ME STHOME TIME TO DISTHCOVER THAT IT WAS MY STHUPER STHPETHIAL TALENT.

PRETTY *THWEET,* HUH?

YEAH. PRETTY... *THWEET.*

HEY. *THITH DOETHN'T* MEAN WE CAN'T GO TO THE CUTE-*THINERA* TOGETHER.

YOU'RE *THTILL* GONNA COME TO THE PARTY AREN'T YOU?

OF COURSE SHE WILL. IT'S NOT LIKE BEING THE *ONLY* PONY THERE WITHOUT A CUTIE MARK WILL BE, LIKE...

...THE MOST EMBARRASSING THING EVER.

HE HE HE HE

WHOA. LOOKS LIKE SOMEPONY'S GOT A DARK CLOUD HANGING OVER HER HEAD.

WHAT'S THE MATTER, KID?

WELL...

GASP

THERE'S A CUTE-CINERA THIS AFTERNOON AND EVERYPONY IN MY CLASS WILL BE THERE AND THEY ALL HAVE THEIR CUTIE MARKS, AND I WANT TO GET MY CUTIE MARK, BUT I'M NO GOOD AT SELLING APPLES BUT I REALLY WANT TO GO TO THE PARTY, BUT HOW CAN I GO TO THE PARTY IF I DON'T HAVE MY CUTIE MARK, WHICH MY BIG SISTER SAYS I'M GONNA GET *EVENTUALLY*, BUT...

...I WANT IT NOOOOOOOOW.

CUTIE MARK? I CAN GET YOU A CUTIE MARK LIKE THAT.

BUT APPLEJACK SAYS THESE THINGS TAKE TIME.

I HAVE TO JUST WAIT FOR IT TO HAPPEN.

WHY WAIT FOR SOMETHING TO HAPPEN WHEN YOU CAN *MAKE* IT HAPPEN?

BUT APPLEJACK SAYS—

HEY, WHO ARE YOU GOING TO LISTEN TO? APPLEJACK? OR THE PONY WHO WAS *FIRST* IN HER CLASS TO GET A CUTIE MARK?

I ALWAYS LIKED FLYING AND ALL. BUT I WAS GOING NOWHERE IN A HURRY. IT WASN'T UNTIL MY VERY FIRST RACE THAT I DISCOVERED A SERIOUS NEED FOR SPEED AND *KAZAM!*

THIS SWEET BABY APPEARED AS FAST AS LIGHTNING!

THAT'S RIGHT. STRETCH THOSE LEGS. GOTTA BE NICE AND LOOSE.

<UNGH>

THE KEY HERE IS TO TRY AS MANY THINGS AS POSSIBLE AS QUICKLY AS POSSIBLE.

ONE OF 'EM IS BOUND TO LEAD TO YOUR CUTIE MARK!

ARE YOU READY?

I'M READY.

I SAID... ARE YOU READY?!

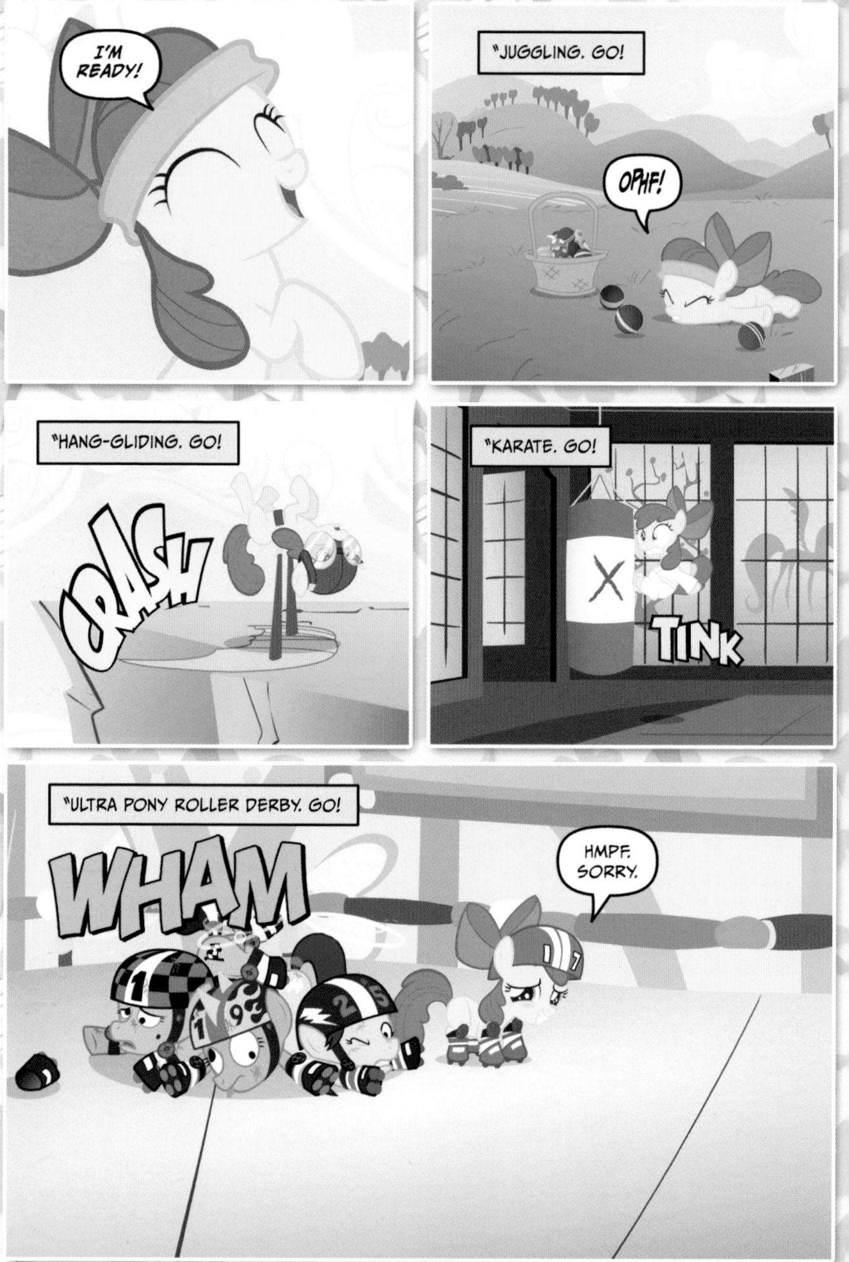
I'M READY!
"JUGGLING. GO!
OPHF!
"HANG-GLIDING. GO!
CRASH
"KARATE. GO!
TINK
"ULTRA PONY ROLLER DERBY. GO!
WHAM
HMPF. SORRY.

TRIED THAT ONE...
TRIED THAT ONE...
TRIED THAT ONE...

I'M DOOMED. DOOMED! I'LL NEVER FIND SOMETHING I'M GOOD AT.

YOU LOOK LIKE YOU'D BE GOOD AT EATING CUPCAKES!

EATING CUPCAKES?

EATING CUPCAKES?

EATING CUPCAKES!

BOING

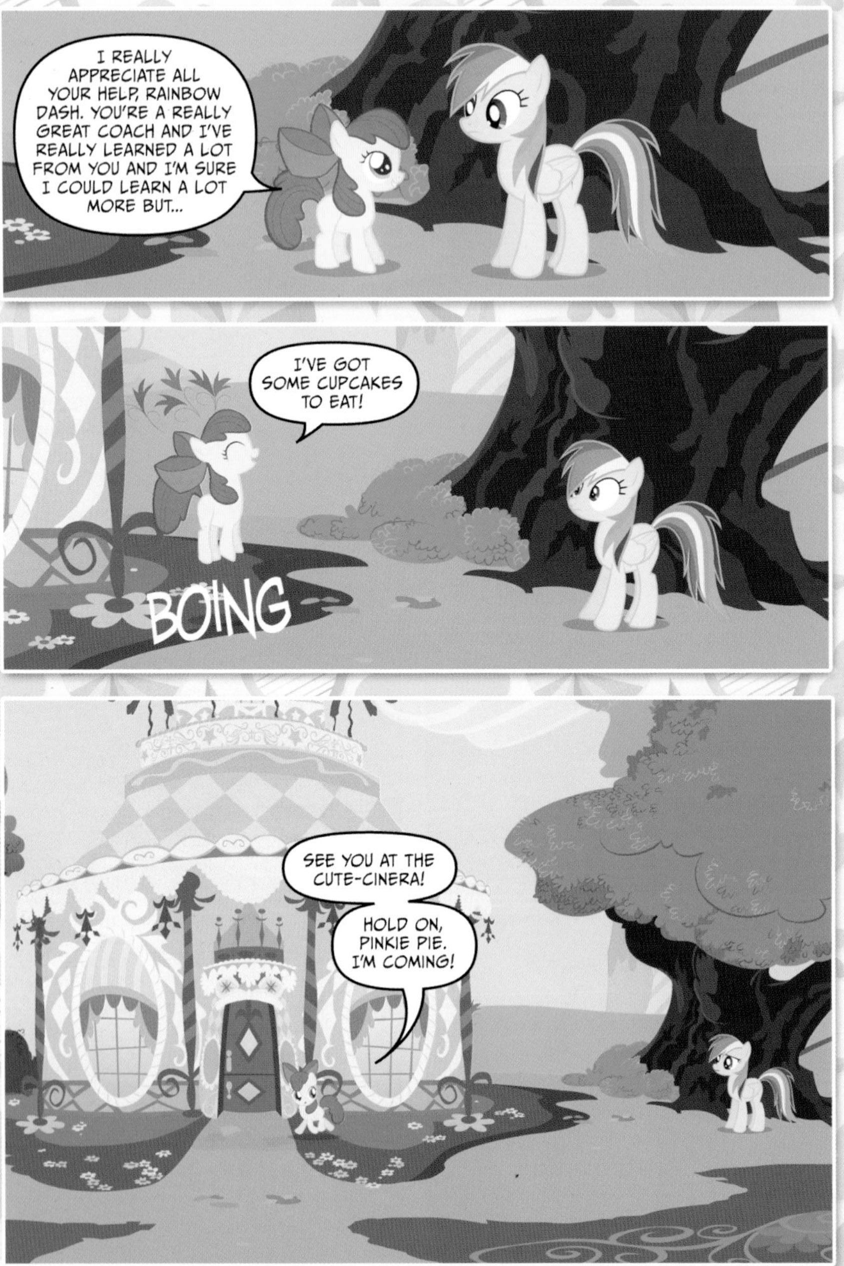
I REALLY APPRECIATE ALL YOUR HELP, RAINBOW DASH. YOU'RE A REALLY GREAT COACH AND I'VE REALLY LEARNED A LOT FROM YOU AND I'M SURE I COULD LEARN A LOT MORE BUT...
I'VE GOT SOME CUPCAKES TO EAT!
BOING
SEE YOU AT THE CUTE-CINERA!
HOLD ON, PINKIE PIE. I'M COMING!

I CAN'T BELIEVE I DIDN'T THINK OF THIS.

A CUPCAKE-EATING CUTIE MARK. IT'S SOOO OBVIOUS.

NOW WHERE ARE THOSE CUPCAKES? I AM READY TO CHOW DOWN!

I DON'T HAVE ANY CUPCAKES.

OH—

BUT YOU LOOK LIKE YOU'D BE GOOD AT HELPING ME MAKE SOME!

I GUESS A MAKING-CUPCAKES CUTIE MARK COULD WORK TOO.

I THINK THEY'RE READY!

POOF

LET'S SEE...

TSSSSSS

HOT! HOT!

OOH, THOSE LOOK MUCH BETTER THAN THE LAST BATCH.

CHOMP
CHOMP

EEURGH!

GUESS I'M NOT CUT OUT TO BE A BAKER, EITHER.

⟨SIGH⟩

I JUST HAVE TO FACE IT. I'M GONNA HAVE A *BLANK FLANK* FOREVER.

WELL WHAT ABOUT THAT?!

WHAT ABOUT WHAT? IS THERE SOMETHING ON MY FLANK?

IS THERE IS THERE IS THERE??

A CUTIE MARK!

IT'S A, UH... A MEASURING CUP?

A MIXING BOWL?

ARE THOSE CUPCAKES? A TOWER OF CUPCAKES MAYBE?

PHWWWW

FLOUR! IT'S FLOUR!

YAY! I GUESSED IT!

WHOA. WHAT'S BEEN GOING ON IN HERE?

WE'VE BEEN MAKING CUPCAKES! WANT TO TRY ONE?

NO, THANK YOU.

NOT THAT THEY DON'T LOOK... DELICIOUS.

TWILIGHT! YOU HAVE TO HELP ME!

WHAT'S THE MATTER?

TIARA'S CUTE-CINERA IS TODAY AND EVERYPONY IN MY CLASS WILL BE THERE AND THEY ALL HAVE THEIR CUTIE MARKS, AND I WANT TO GET MY CUTIE MARK, BUT I'M NO GOOD AT SELLING APPLES, OR HANG-GLIDING OR MAKING CUPCAKES, BUT I WANT TO GO TO THE PARTY, BUT HOW CAN I GO TO THE PARTY IF I DON'T HAVE MY CUTIE MARK, WHICH PINKIE PIE SAYS I CAN'T JUST "MAKE APPEAR", BUT I *NEED* IT TO APPEAR...

...RIGHT NOOOOOOOOW.

ERR, I DON'T FOLLOW. HOW CAN *I* HELP YOU?

YOU CAN USE YOUR MAGIC TO MAKE MY CUTIE MARK APPEAR.

OH NO, APPLE BLOOM.

A CUTIE MARK IS SOMETHING THAT A PONY HAS TO DISCOVER FOR HERSELF.

PLEASE, TWILIGHT. JUST TRY.

I'M SORRY BUT—

OH, PLEASE. PLEASE. PLEASE. PLEASE. *PLEEEEASE.*

I'M SORRY SWEETIE, BUT I TOLD YOU...

...NOT EVEN MAGIC CAN MAKE A CUTIE MARK APPEAR BEFORE ITS TIME.

IT'S HOPELESS. HOPELESS!

I JUST WON'T GO TO THE PARTY. I CAN'T GO.

EVERYONE WILL JUST LAUGH AT ME AND MAKE FUN OF ME AND CALL ME NAMES.

IT'LL BE THE WORST NIGHT OF MY LIFE!

I'M SURE IT WON'T BE AS BAD AS ALL THAT.

FORGET IT. THERE IS NO WAY I'M GOING TO THAT—

—PARTY.

?!

ZIP

HOW COULD I HAVE FORGOTTEN THE TIME?

HOW COULD I HAVE FORGOTTEN PINKY PIE WAS HOSTING THE PARTY?

DONK

DON'T FORGET YOUR PARTY HAT, *FORGETTY FORGETTERSEN!*

I HAVE TO GET OUT OF HERE BEFORE ANYPONY SEES ME.

ZIP

OKAY, APPLE BLOOM. ALMOST THERE.

BONK

APPLE BLOOM, YOU MADE IT!

AFTER I HEARD ABOUT TWIST, I WAS AFRAID YOU WOULDN'T SHOW UP.

SURE AM GLAD YOU CAME TO YOUR SENSES ABOUT THIS WHOLE CUTIE MARK THING.

THESE THINGS HAPPEN WHEN THESE THINGS ARE SUPPOSED TO HAPPEN.

TRYING TO RUSH IT'LL JUST DRIVE YOU CRAZY.

LOOKS LIKE YOUR FRIENDS WANNA TALK TO YOU.

WELL, WELL, WELL...

I'LL LET YOU BE.

YANK

‹HMPF›

LOOK WHO'S HERE.

NICE OUTFIT.

JUST SOMETHING I, UH, PULLED TOGETHER *LAST MINUTE*.

HE HE HE HE

IT REALLY SHOWS OFF YOUR CUTIE MARK.

OH. WAIT. THAT'S RIGHT. *YOU* DON'T HAVE ONE.

I HAVE A CUTIE MARK.

WHAT?! SINCE WHEN?

SINCE EARLIER TODAY.

OH REALLY?!

LET'S SEE IT!

I SHOULDN'T. I COULDN'T. MY CUTIE MARK IS SO UNBELIEVABLY AMAZING...

...I'M AFRAID THAT IF I SHOW IT OFF EVERYONE WILL START PAYING ATTENTION TO ME...

...INSTEAD OF *YOU.*

OUTSHINED AT YOUR OWN CUTE-CINERA. CAN YOU IMAGINE HOW EMBARRASSING THAT WOULD BE?

ERR, FORGET IT. I DIDN'T REALLY WANT TO SEE IT ANYWAY.

OKAY, WELL, I'M GONNA GO MINGLE. ENJOY YOUR PARTY.

UUUUURRRK

TRIP

WHAM

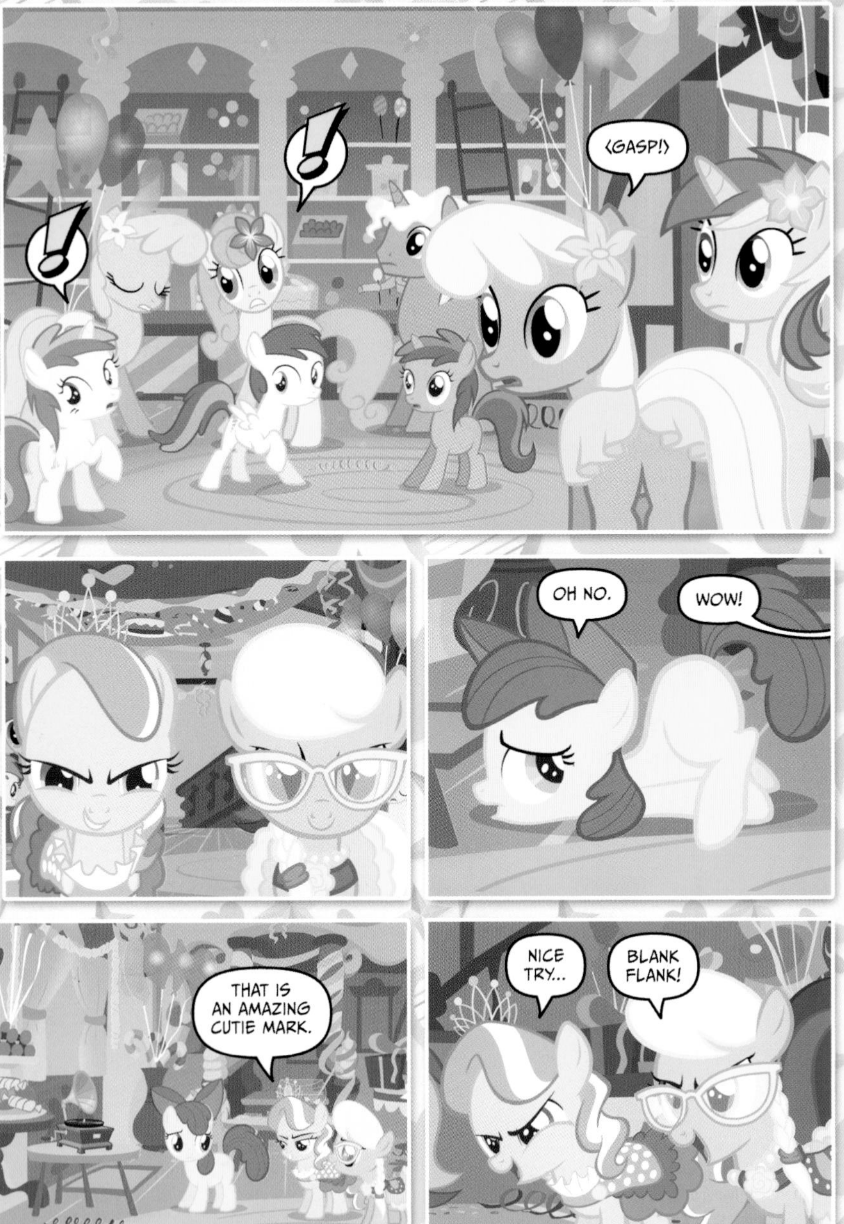
!
!
<GASP!>
OH NO.
WOW!
THAT IS AN AMAZING CUTIE MARK.
NICE TRY...
BLANK FLANK!

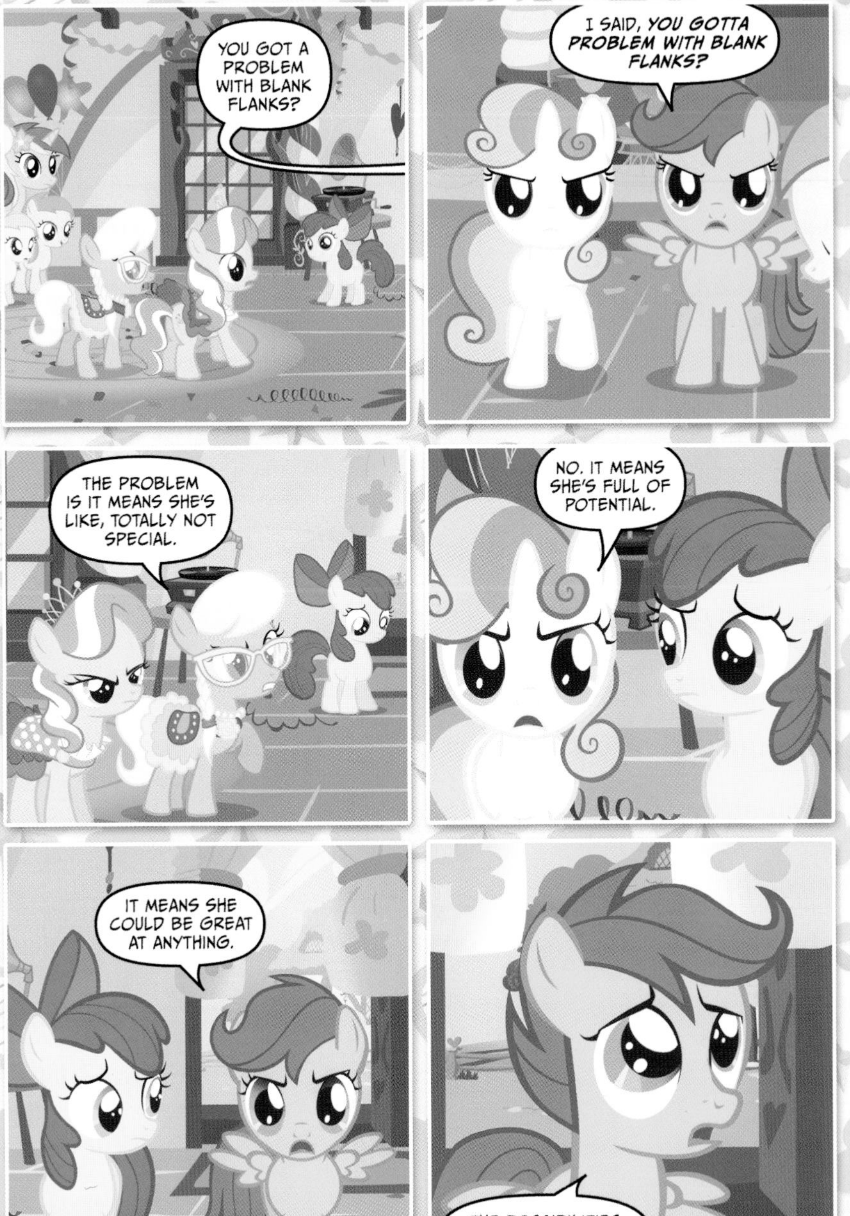
YOU GOT A PROBLEM WITH BLANK FLANKS?
I SAID, *YOU GOTTA PROBLEM WITH BLANK FLANKS?*
THE PROBLEM IS IT MEANS SHE'S LIKE, TOTALLY NOT SPECIAL.
NO. IT MEANS SHE'S FULL OF POTENTIAL.
IT MEANS SHE COULD BE GREAT AT ANYTHING.
THE POSSIBILITIES ARE... ***LIKE, ENDLESS.***

SHE COULD BE A GREAT SCIENTIST, OR AN AMAZING ARTIST...

...OR A FAMOUS WRITER...

...SHE COULD EVEN BE MAYOR OF PONYVILLE SOMEDAY!

AND SHE'S NOT STUCK BEING STUCK-UP LIKE YOU TWO!

HEHEHE

HAHA

HEY! THIS IS *MY* PARTY. WHY ARE YOU TWO ON *HER* SIDE?

BECAUSE...

YOU DON'T HAVE YOUR CUTIE MARKS, EITHER!

I THOUGHT I WAS THE ONLY ONE.

WE THOUGHT *WE* WERE THE ONLY TWO.

I FOR ONE THINK YOU ARE THREE VERY LUCKY FILLIES.

LUCKY? HOW CAN *THEY* BE LUCKY?

*THEY* STILL GET TO EXPERIENCE THE THRILL OF DISCOVERING WHO THEY ARE...

...AND WHAT THEY ARE MEANT TO BE.

AND THEY'VE GOT ALL THE TIME IN THE WORLD TO FIGURE IT OUT.

NOT JUST AN AFTERNOON.

WOW APPLE BLOOM!

DO YOU REALLY THINK YOU CAN BE MAYOR?

I WISH I COULD BE A SCIENTIST!

MAYBE I GOT MY CUTIE MARK TOO SOON...

HEY! WHAT'S EVERYBODY DOING?

THIS IS *MY* PARTY! EVERYPONY'S SUPPOSED TO BE PAYING ATTENTION TO ME!

WHATEVER. WE STILL THINK YOU'RE LOSERS.

RIGHT, TIARA?

NOT NOW, SILVER SPOON.

NAME'S SCOOTALOO.

AND I'M SWEETIE BELLE.

APPLE BLOOM.

MAYBE THE PARTY WASN'T SO BAD AFTER ALL.

SO I WAS THINKING. NOW THAT WE'RE FRIENDS...

...I MEAN, WE ARE FRIENDS, RIGHT?

HOW COULD WE NOT BE? WE'RE TOTALLY ALIKE. WE DON'T HAVE CUTIE MARKS...

DIAMOND TIARA AND SILVER SPOON DRIVE US CRAZY...

TOTALLY CRAZY!

HE HE

HE HE

NOW THAT WE'RE FRIENDS, WHAT IF THE THREE OF US WORKED *TOGETHER* TO FIND OUT WHO WE ARE...

...AND WHAT WE'RE SUPPOSED TO BE?

OOH. OOH. WE COULD FORM OUR OWN SECRET SOCIETY.

I'M LIKING THIS IDEA.

A SECRET SOCIETY. YEAH.

WE'LL NEED A GOOD NAME FOR IT THOUGH.

THE CUTIE MARK THREE?

THE CUTE-TASTICALLY FANTASTICS?

HOW ABOUT...

THE CUTIE MARK CRUSADERS?!

IT'S PERFECT!

THIS IS GOING TO BE SO GREAT.

WHAT DO YOU SAY WE CELEBRATE WITH SOME OF THESE DELICIOUS CUPCAKES?

NOT THE CUPCAKES! TRUST ME.

LET'S SEE IF THERE ARE ANY COOKIES!

YEAH!

COME ON!

"DEAREST PRINCESS CELESTIA, I AM HAPPY TO REPORT THAT ONE OF YOUR YOUNGEST SUBJECTS...

"...HAS LEARNED A VALUABLE LESSON ABOUT FRIENDSHIP.

"SOMETIMES THE THING YOU THINK WILL CAUSE YOU TO LOSE FRIENDS AND FEEL LEFT OUT..."

...CAN ACTUALLY BE THE THING THAT HELPS YOU MAKE YOUR CLOSEST FRIENDS AND REALIZE HOW SPECIAL YOU ARE...

NOT THE END!

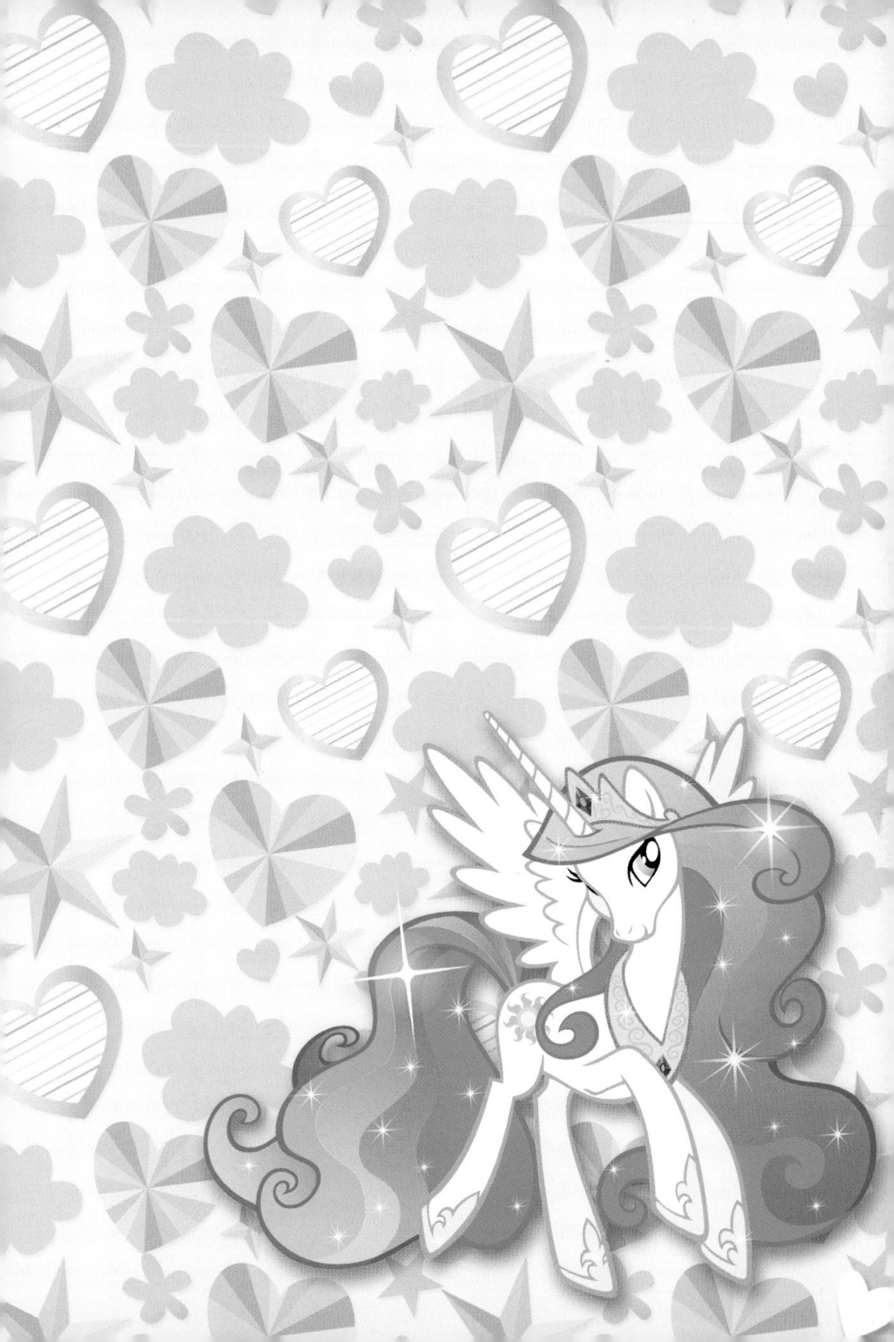

# THE CUTIE MARK CHRONICLES

ARE YOU SURE ABOUT THIS, SCOOTALOO? I'VE NEVER EVEN HEARD OF A PONY ZIPLINING BEFORE.

NEITHER HAVE I.

BUT SPIKE TOLD ME IT WAS *AWESOME*.

HOP

XOINK

YANK

HEY, WE'RE SLOWING DOWN!

YEAH!

AAHHH!

CRACKLE

THE ROPE'S BURNING IT COULD—

SNAP

AAHHH!

WHAM

SEE ANYTHING?

TREE SAP AND PINE NEEDLES, BUT NO CUTIE MARK.

PLAN B?

YEAH.

YOU KNOW WHERE WE CAN FIND A CANNON AT THIS HOUR?

AW, IT'S NO USE.

NO MATTER WHAT WE TRY, WE ALWAYS END UP WITHOUT OUR CUTIE MARKS.

AND SURPRISINGLY OFTEN COVERED IN TREE SAP.

MAYBE WE SHOULD DO SOMETHING LESS DANGEROUS... LIKE PILLOW TESTING OR FLOWER SNIFFING—

THIS TOWN IS FULL OF PONIES WHO HAVE THEIR CUTIE MARKS!

WHY DON'T WE ASK THEM HOW THEY DID IT?

THAT'S A GREAT, SAFE IDEA!

YEAH! AND WE CAN START WITH THE COOLEST PONY IN PONYVILLE!

RAINBOW DASH!

FRRRRMMMMMM

GASP!

SKREEEEE

SKREEEEEEEE

PHEW!

GET BACK HERE, YOU THIEVING' VARMINTS!

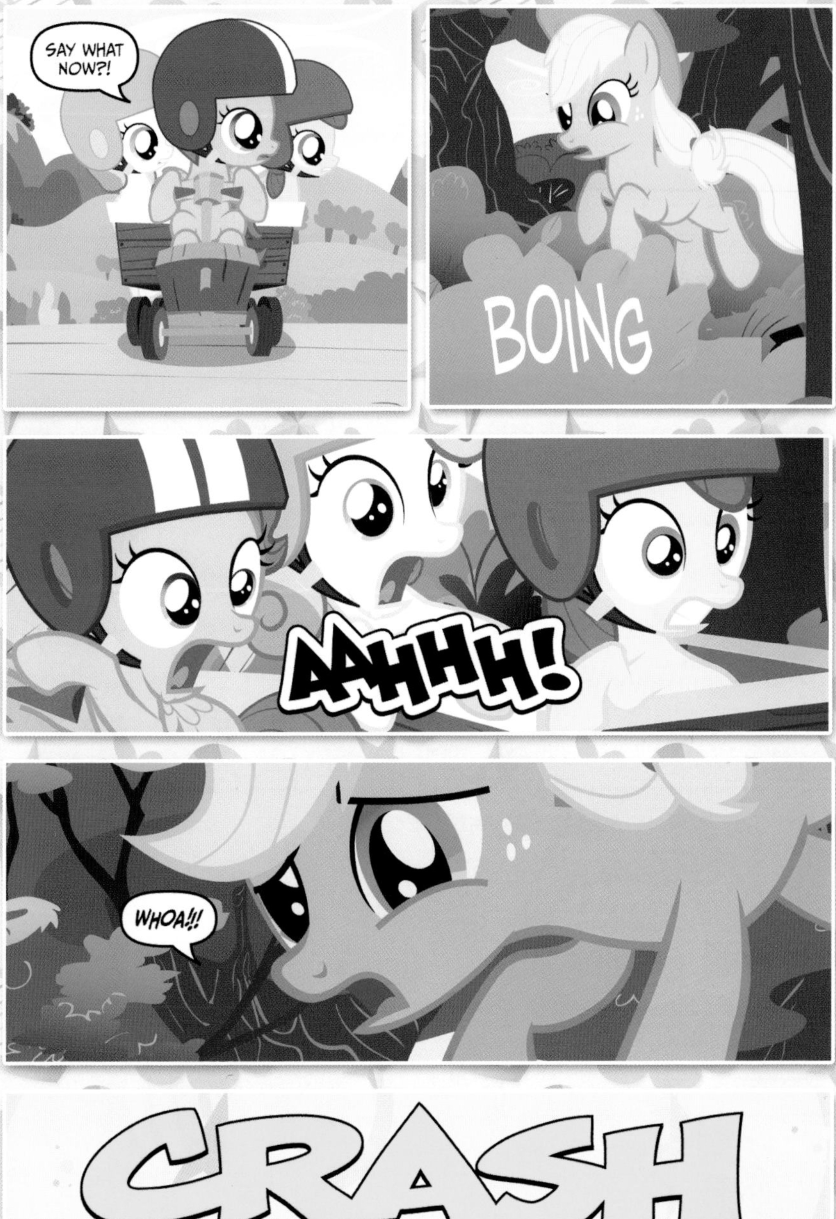

SAY WHAT NOW?!
BOING
AAHHH!
WHOA!!!
CRASH

APPLE BLOOM?!

HEY SIS! HOW DID YOU GET YOUR CUTIE MARK?

I NEVER TOLD YOU THAT STORY?

HEY! I THOUGHT WE WERE GOING TO ASK RAINBOW DASH!

WE NEED ALL THE HELP WE CAN GET!

WHY SHOOT, I WAS JUST A LITTLE FILLY. EVEN LITTLER THAN Y'ALL...

"I DIDN'T WANT TO SPEND MY LIFE ON A MUDDY OL' APPLE FARM.

"I WANTED TO LIVE THE SOPHISTICATED LIFE...

"...LIKE MY AUNT AND UNCLE ORANGE.

"SO I SET OUT TO TRY MY LUCK IN THE BIG CITY...

"...MANEHATTAN!

"THE MOST COSMOPOLITAN CITY IN ALL OF EQUESTRIA!"

"I KNEW I'D FIND WHO I WAS MEANT TO BE IN *MANEHATTAN*..."

KNOCK KNOCK

AUNT ORANGE! UNCLE ORANGE!

THANK Y'ALL SO MUCH FOR LETTIN' ME STAY!

"Y'ALL!" ISN'T SHE JUST THE LIVING END?

HOW QUAINT!

DON'T WORRY, WE'LL HAVE YOU ACTING LIKE A TRUE *MANEHATTANITE* IN NO TIME!

AND HOW ARE YOU FINDING GOOD OL' MANEHATTAN?

OH, IT'S SIMPLY DIVINE!

VERY WELL SAID, MY DEAR.

SOON...

ALTHOUGH, I MUST ADMIT THE CITY NOISE TOOK SOME GETTING USED TO.

WHERE I'M FROM, NIGHTS ARE SO QUIET YOU SELDOM HEAR A PEEP UNTIL THE ROOSTERS WAKE YOU!

THE... WHAT?

I SAY, MY DEAR, WHAT IN THE WORLD IS A "ROOSTER"?

WHAT'S HE TALKING ABOUT?

WHAT DO I SAY?

I DON'T WANNA LOOK LIKE A FOOL!

DINGDINGDING

DINNER IS SERVED.

THANK GOODNESS! BEIN' A CITY PONY'S HARD WORK!

I'M SO HUNGRY I COULD EAT A— —OH.

ARLY THE NEXT DAY...

COCK-A-DOODLE-DOO.

⟨SIGH.⟩

I WONDER WHAT GRANNY SMITH AND BIG MCINTOSH ARE UP TO.

I BET THEY'RE APPLEBUCKIN' THEIR WAY THROUGH THE RED DELICIOUS TREES.

OOOH, WHAT I WOULDN'T GIVE FOR JUST ONE BITE...

"I NEVER FELT SO HOMESICK IN ALL MY DAYS AS I DID RIGHT THEN...

PLINK

"IT WAS AMAZING. A RAINBOW POINTING RIGHT BACK TO... HOME.

"IN THAT MOMENT IT ALL BECAME CLEAR.

"I KNEW RIGHT THEN JUST WHO I WAS S'POSED TO BE..."

CLOPCLOPCLOP

WELCOME HOME, DEAR!

POOF

THAT'S WHEN THIS HERE APPEARED.

I BEEN HAPPILY WORKIN' THE FARM EVER SINCE.

*SNAP*

THERE THEY ARE!

GET BACK HERE, YOU THIEVIN' VARMINTS!!

AWWW, THAT WAS SUCH A SWEET STORY!

SWEET? TRY SAPPY! BLECH!

FRRRRMMMMMM

COME ON, WE'VE GOT TO FIND RAINBOW DASH AND HEAR THE COOL WAY TO GET A CUTIE MARK!

WHUMPH

AAHHH!

LOOK OUT!

SCREECH

WHOA!

AHHHH!

EEEEEEE!

WHAM

QUACK QUACK QUACK

ALRIGHT, LITTLE ONES, THIS WAY... THIS WAY.

YOU REALLY SHOULD BE MORE CAREFUL. SOMEPONY COULD GET HURT.

WHY ARE YOU IN SUCH A HURRY ANYWAY?

WE'RE TRYING TO FIND RAINBOW DASH SO WE CAN HEAR HOW SHE EARNED HER CUTIE MARK.

OH! THAT WOULD BE INTERESTING!

YOU KNOW, I WOULDN'T HAVE GOTTEN *MY* CUTIE MARK IF IT WEREN'T FOR HER.

RAINBOW DASH? REALLY?

OH YES! IT ALL STARTED AT SUMMER FLIGHT CAMP...

"YOU'D NEVER GUESS, BUT WHEN I WAS LITTLE, I WAS VERY SHY."

"AND A WEAK FLYER, TOO."

OH!

DUFF

HAHAHA! NICE GOING, *KLUTZ-ERSHY!* THEY OUGHTA GROUND YOU PERMANENTLY!

HA! MY BABY BROTHER CAN FLY BETTER THAN YOU!

"IT WAS THE MOST HUMILIATING MOMENT OF MY LIFE.

"AND THEN, OUT OF NOWHERE..."

LEAVE HER ALONE!

OOOOOH! WHAT ARE YOU GONNA DO, RAINBOW *CRASH?!*

KEEP MAKING FUN OF HER AND FIND OUT!

YOU THINK YOU'RE SUCH A BIG SHOT? WHY DON'T YOU PROVE IT!

WHATTAYA HAVE IN MIND?

"SO WE RACED."

START

YOU'RE GOING DOWN.

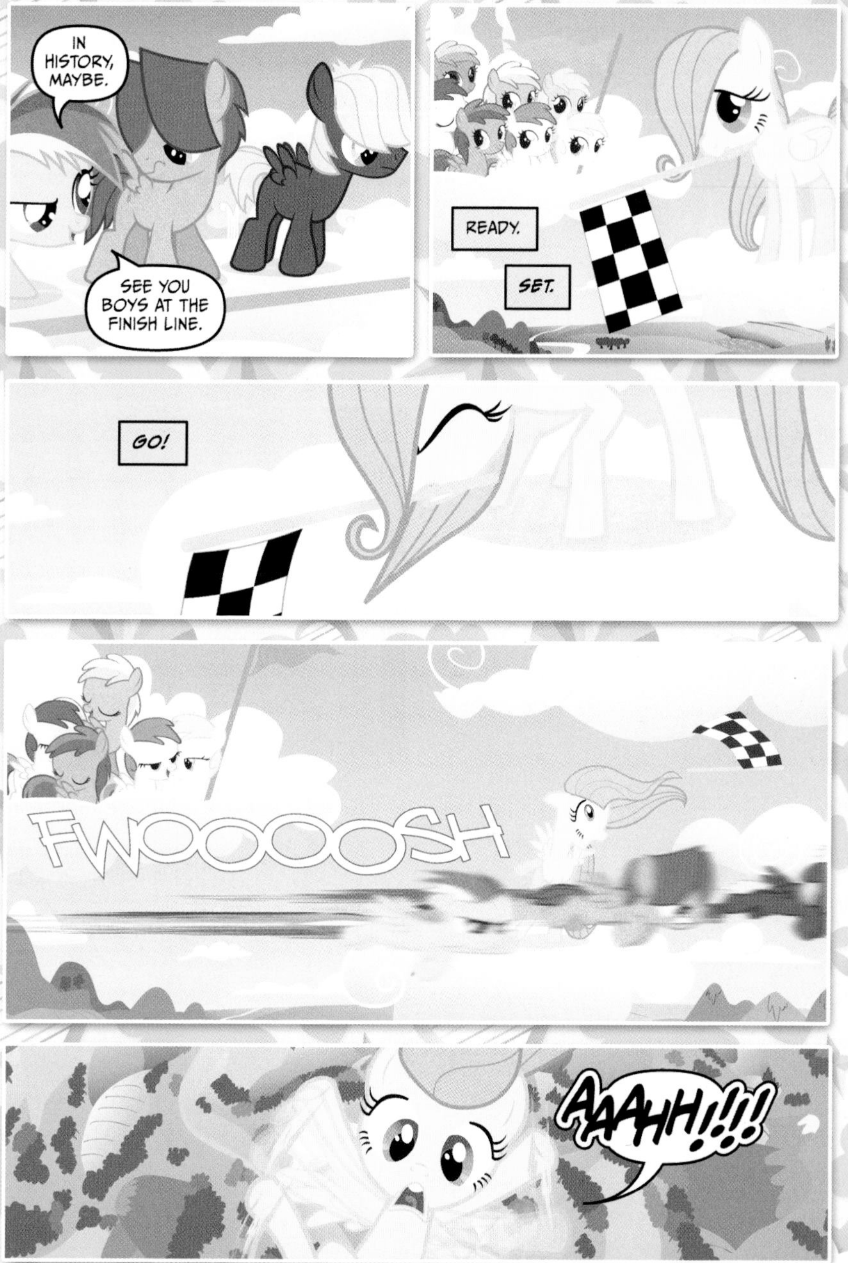
IN HISTORY, MAYBE.
SEE YOU BOYS AT THE FINISH LINE.
READY.
SET.
GO!
FWOOOOSH
AAAHH!!!!

AAHHH!

POOOFT

HUH?!

"I HAD NEVER SEEN SUCH BEAUTIFUL CREATURES.

"BUTTERFLIES DON'T FLY AS HIGH AS MY CLOUD HOME, AND I HAD NEVER BEEN NEAR THE GROUND BEFORE.

WHUMP

"THE LOUD NOISE SCARED THE ANIMALS."

SHHHH. IT'S OKAY.

YOU CAN COME OUT.

EVERYTHING'S OK.

THERE'S NOTHING TO BE AFRAID OF.

"SOMEHOW I HAD THE ABILITY TO COMMUNICATE WITH THE ANIMALS ON A DIFFERENT LEVEL..."

POOF

WAIT WAIT WAIT! WHAT HAPPENED TO RAINBOW DASH?

WHAT ABOUT THE RACE?!

OH. WELL, I WASN'T THERE SO... I DON'T REALLY KNOW WHAT HAPPENED.

COME ON, CRUSADERS, WE'VE GOT TO FIND HER!

MAYBE MY SISTER KNOWS WHERE SHE IS.

BYE FLUTTERSHY!

BYE GIRLS!

**B**UT IT'S NOT THAT EASY...

HOW DID WE GET ROPED INTO *THIS*? WE'LL NEVER HEAR RAINBOW DASH'S STORY.

ARE YOU GIRLS STILL OBSESSING OVER YOUR CUTIE MARKS?

OF COURSE! MOST OF THE FILLIES AT SCHOOL ALREADY HAVE THEIRS!

I KNOW HOW YOU FEEL. FOR THE LONGEST TIME, I COULDN'T FIGURE OUT WHY I DIDN'T HAVE MINE...

"I WAS MAKING COSTUMES FOR A MUSICAL..."

WELL DONE, RARITY. YOUR COSTUMES ARE VERY NICE.

NICE?!

NICE? THEY NEED TO BE *SPECTACULAR!*

AND THE PERFORMANCE IS TOMORROW!

"I TRIED EVERY TRICK I COULD THINK OF, BUT NOTHING SEEMED TO WORK.

"THE COSTUMES JUST WEREN'T RIGHT. AND THE PLAY OPENED THAT NIGHT!

MAYBE I'M NOT MEANT TO BE A FASHIONISTA AFTER ALL...

WHAT'S GOING ON?!

"I HAD NO IDEA WHERE MY HORN WAS TAKING ME..."

"...BUT UNICORN MAGIC DOESN'T HAPPEN WITHOUT A REASON.

"I KNEW THIS HAD TO DO WITH MY LOVE OF FASHION...

"...AND MAYBE EVEN MY CUTIE MARK.

WHAMMM

"I KNEW THAT THIS WAS...

"...MY DESTINY."

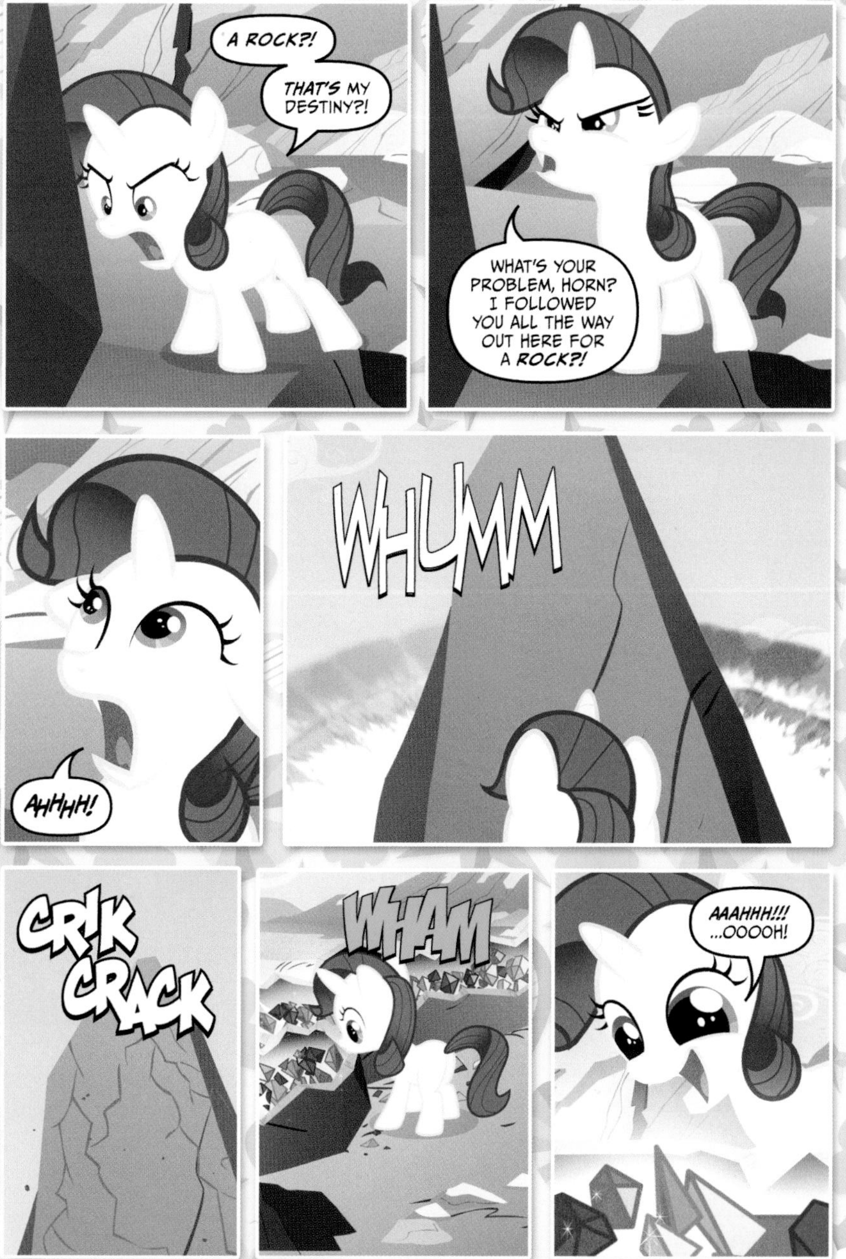
A ROCK?!
THAT'S MY DESTINY?!
WHAT'S YOUR PROBLEM, HORN? I FOLLOWED YOU ALL THE WAY OUT HERE FOR A *ROCK?!*
AHHHH!
WHUMM
CRIK CRACK
WHAM
AAAHHH!!! ...OOOOH!

"THE JEWELS DID JUST THE TRICK."

SPECTACULAR!

OOOOOHHH!

"I WAS SO PROUD."

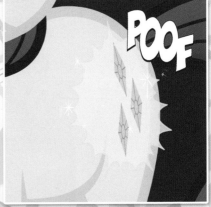

POOF

AAAAAHHH!!!!

THESE NAMBY-PAMBY STORIES AREN'T GETTING US ANY CLOSER TO OUR CUTIE MARKS!

THEY'RE ALL ABOUT "FINDING WHO YOU REALLY ARE" AND BORING STUFF LIKE THAT!

YES, SCOOTALOO! THAT'S *EXACTLY*—

COME ON, GIRLS!

WE NEED ACTION!

WE NEED RAINBOW DASH!

AS A YOUNG FILLY IN CANTERLOT...

...I ALWAYS WANTED TO GO TO THE SUMMER SUN CELEBRATION...

THUD

"...WHERE PRINCESS CELESTIA RAISES THE SUN.

"...AND I SAW THE MOST AMAZING, MOST WONDERFUL THING I'VE EVER SEEN."

OOOOH!

AHHHH!

WOO-HOO! HOORAY!

SHE'S INCREDIBLE!

DRIP DRIP

〈HNNNNNN〉

〈YAWN〉

WE DON'T HAVE ALL DAY.

"I KNEW IT WAS THE MOST IMPORTANT DAY OF MY LIFE.

〈HNNNNNNN〉

"THAT MY ENTIRE FUTURE WOULD BE AFFECTED BY THE OUTCOME OF THIS DAY!"

"AND I WAS ABOUT TO BLOW IT!"

I'M SORRY I WASTED YOUR TIME.

WHUMM

ZAP

ZOOT

BLART

⟨YAWN⟩

AAAAHHH!!!

ZZZKT

ZZZKT

?

TWILIGHT SPARKLE, YOU HAVE A VERY SPECIAL GIFT.

I DON'T THINK I'VE EVER COME ACROSS A UNICORN WITH YOUR RAW ABILITIES.

HUH?!

BUT YOU NEED TO LEARN TO TAME THESE ABILITIES THROUGH FOCUSED STUDY.

HUH?!

TWILIGHT SPARKLE, I'D LIKE TO MAKE YOU MY OWN PERSONAL PROTEGE HERE AT THE SCHOOL.

HUH?!

WELL...?

YES!!!!

ONE MORE THING, TWILIGHT...

MY CUTIE MARK! YES YES YES YES YES YES YES YES YES YES...

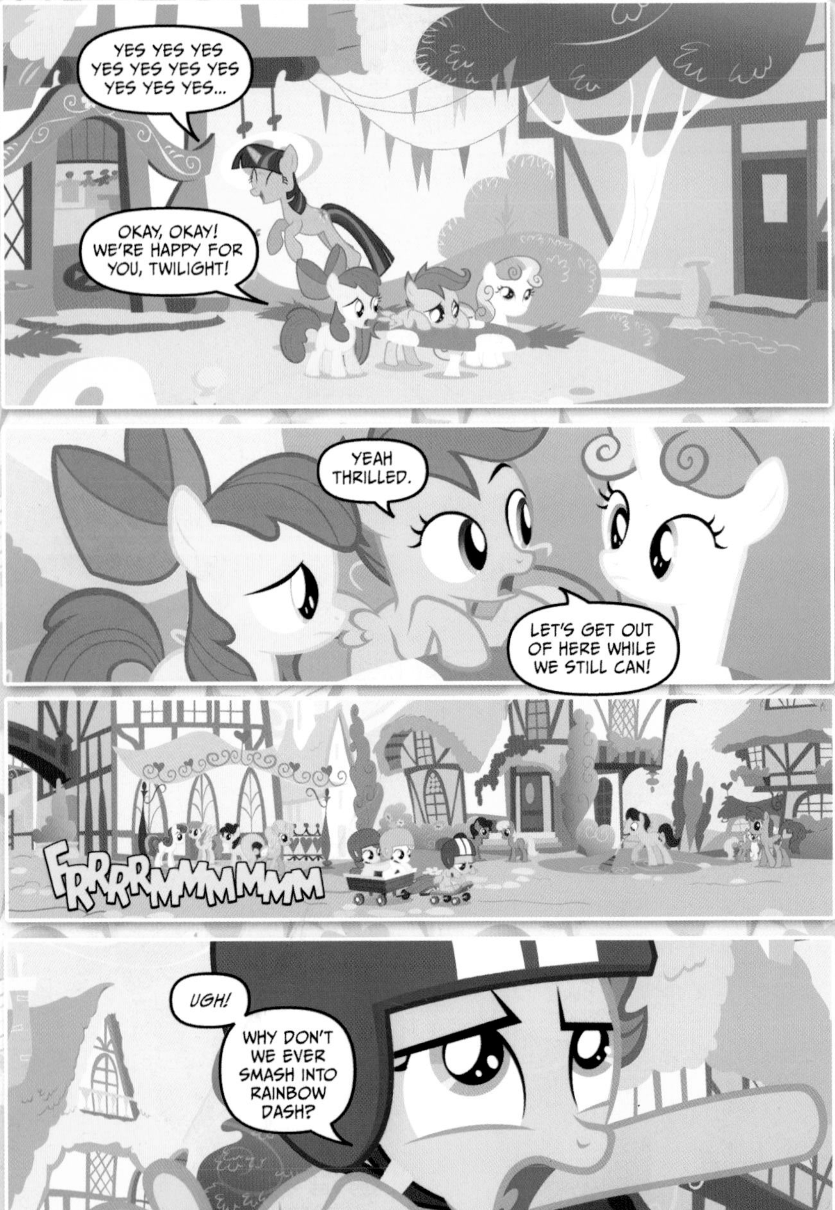
YES YES YES YES YES YES YES YES YES YES...
OKAY, OKAY! WE'RE HAPPY FOR YOU, TWILIGHT!
YEAH THRILLED.
LET'S GET OUT OF HERE WHILE WE STILL CAN!
FRRRRMMMMMMM
UGH!
WHY DON'T WE EVER SMASH INTO RAINBOW DASH?

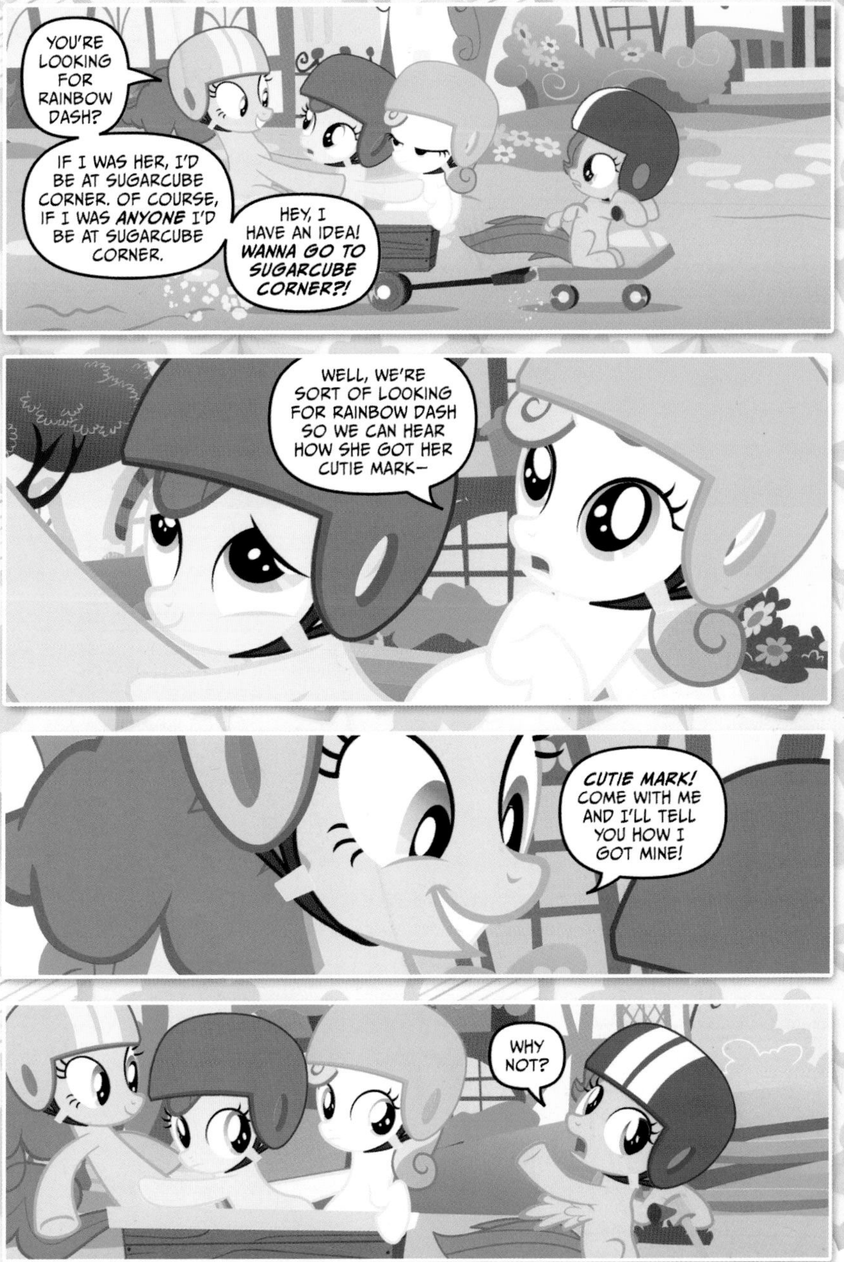
YOU'RE LOOKING FOR RAINBOW DASH?
IF I WAS HER, I'D BE AT SUGARCUBE CORNER. OF COURSE, IF I WAS *ANYONE* I'D BE AT SUGARCUBE CORNER.
HEY, I HAVE AN IDEA! ***WANNA GO TO SUGARCUBE CORNER?!***
WELL, WE'RE SORT OF LOOKING FOR RAINBOW DASH SO WE CAN HEAR HOW SHE GOT HER CUTIE MARK–
***CUTIE MARK!*** COME WITH ME AND I'LL TELL YOU HOW I GOT MINE!
WHY NOT?

"MY SISTERS AND I WERE RAISED ON A ROCK FARM OUTSIDE OF PONYVILLE.

"WE SPENT OUR DAYS WORKING THE FIELDS...

"THERE WAS NO TALKING. THERE WAS NO SMILING. THERE WERE ONLY ROCKS.

"WE WERE IN THE SOUTH FIELD, PREPARING TO ROTATE THE ROCKS TO THE EAST FIELD, WHEN ALL OF A SUDDEN..."

WHAM

"I'D NEVER FELT JOY LIKE THAT BEFORE. IT FELT SO GOOD I JUST WANTED TO KEEP SMILING FOREVER.

"AND I WANTED EVERYONE I KNEW TO SMILE, TOO."

"BUT RAINBOWS DON'T COME ALONG THAT OFTEN. I WONDERED HOW ELSE COULD I CREATE SOME SMILES..."

WE'D BETTER HARVEST THE ROCKS FROM THE SOUTH FIELD.

PINKAMENA DIANE PIE? IS THAT YOU?

MOM! I NEED YOU AND DAD AND THE SISTERS TO COME IN HERE, QUICK!

?!

SURPRISE!

YOU LIKE IT? IT'S CALLED "A PARTY"!

〈GASP!〉

OH, YOU *DON'T* LIKE IT.

YOU LIKE IT!

I'M SO HAPPY!

POOF

AND THAT'S HOW EQUESTRIA WAS MADE!

WHA... HUH—

LOOK, WE'RE HERE!

MAYBE ON THE WAY HOME I CAN TELL YOU THE STORY OF HOW I GOT MY CUTIE MARK.

IT'S A GEM!

COME ON. SHE'S JUST BEING PINKIE PIE.

RAINBOW DASH! YOU'RE HERE!

I HEAR YOU'RE LOOKIN' FOR MY CUTIE MARK STORY.

YOU HAVE NO IDEA WHAT I'VE BEEN THROUGH TODAY TO HEAR THAT STORY!

IT ALL HAPPENED DURING THE RACE AT FLIGHT CAMP...

"...WHERE I STOOD ALONE AGAINST ALL ODDS TO DEFEND FLUTTERSHY'S HONOR..."

**FWIP**

**AAHHH!**

**WOOOOSH**

WOOOOOSH

"I'D NEVER FLOWN LIKE *THIS* BEFORE!

"THE FREEDOM WAS UNLIKE ANYTHING I'D EVER FELT.

"THE SPEED.

"THE ADRENALINE.

"THE WIND IN MY MANE... *I LIKED IT...*"

"...A LOT!"

BAM

LATER, RAINBOW CRASH!

"TURNS OUT THE ONLY THING I LIKED MORE THAN FLYING FAST...

HEY!

"...WAS WINNING."

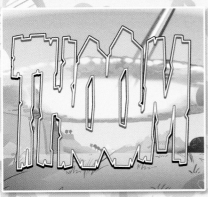

"MOST PEOPLE THOUGHT THE SONIC RAINBOOM WAS JUST AN OLD MARE'S TALE.

"BUT THAT DAY, THE DAY I DISCOVERED RACING, I PROVED THAT THE LEGENDS WERE TRUE.

"I MADE THE IMPOSSIBLE HAPPEN!"

HOORAY!

POOF

AND THAT, LITTLE ONES, IS HOW YOU EARN A CUTIE MARK.

WHOOOOAAAH...

WAIT A SECOND... I HEARD THAT EXPLOSION! AND I SAW THE RAINBOW, TOO!

RAINBOW DASH, IF YOU HADN'T SCARED THE ANIMALS, I NEVER WOULD HAVE LEARNED I COULD COMMUNICATE WITH THEM AND GOTTEN MY CUTIE MARK!

I HEARD THAT BOOM. AND RIGHT AFTERWARDS THERE WAS THIS AMAZING RAINBOW THAT TAUGHT ME TO SMILE!

WHEN I GOT MY CUTIE MARK, I SAW A RAINBOW THAT POINTED ME HOME.

I BET IT WAS YOUR SONIC *RAINBOOM*!

THERE WAS AN EXPLOSION I COULD NEVER EXPLAIN WHEN I GOT *MY CUTIE MARK*!

THIS IS UNCANNY!

IF THAT EXPLOSION DIDN'T HAPPEN WHEN IT DID, I WOULD HAVE BLOWN MY ENTRANCE EXAM!

RAINBOW DASH, I THINK YOU HELPED ME EARN MY CUTIE MARK, TOO!

WE *ALL* OWE OUR CUTIE MARKS TO YOU!

DO YOU REALIZE WHAT THIS MEANS?

ALL OF US HAD A SPECIAL CONNECTION BEFORE WE EVEN MET!

WE'VE BEEN BFFS FOREVER AND WE DIDN'T EVEN KNOW IT!

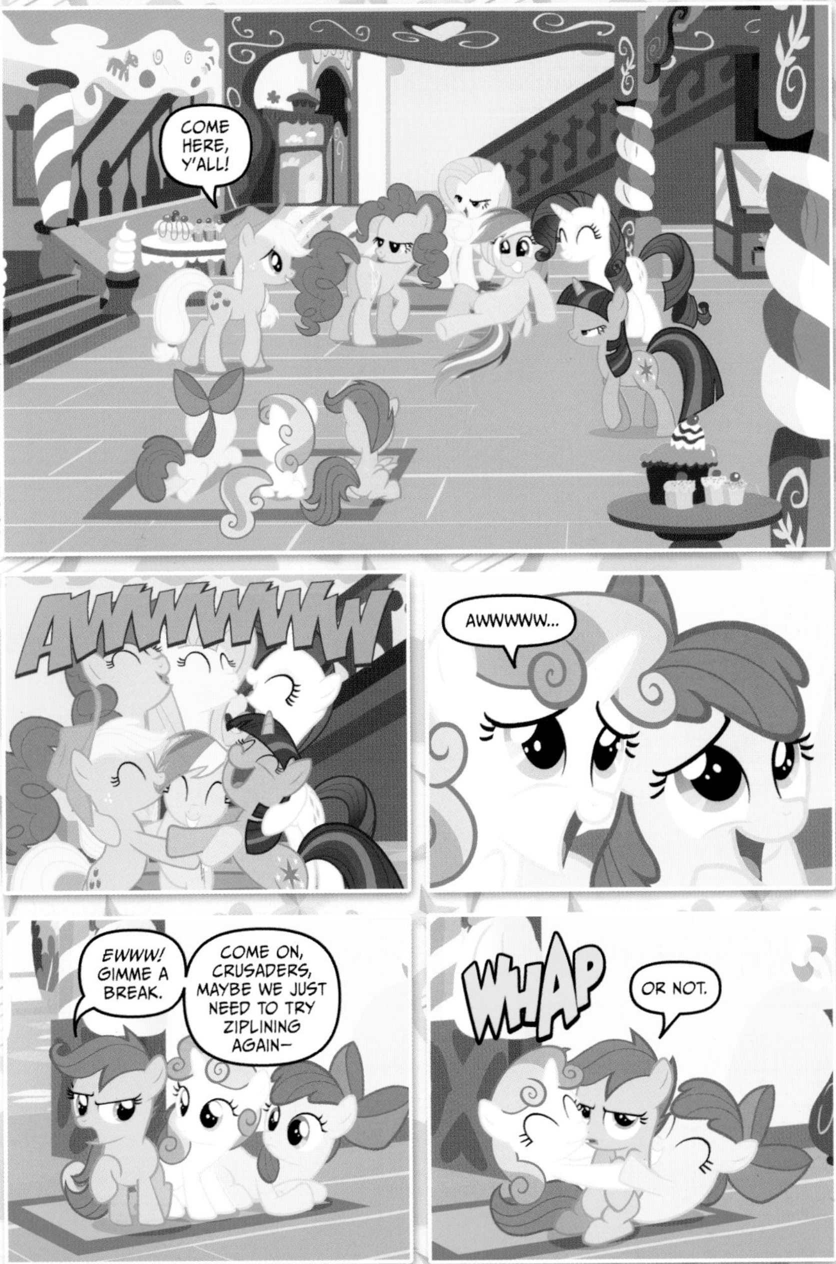
COME HERE, Y'ALL!
AWWWWWWW
AWWWWW...
EWWW! GIMME A BREAK.
COME ON, CRUSADERS, MAYBE WE JUST NEED TO TRY ZIPLINING AGAIN–
WHAP
OR NOT.

"DEAR PRINCESS CELESTIA, TODAY I LEARNED SOMETHING AMAZING."

EVERYPONY EVERYWHERE HAS A SPECIAL, MAGICAL CONNECTION WITH HER FRIENDS, MAYBE EVEN BEFORE SHE'S MET THEM.

IF YOU'RE FEELING LONELY AND YOU'RE STILL SEARCHING FOR YOUR TRUE FRIENDS, JUST LOOK UP IN THE SKY.

"WHO KNOWS, MAYBE YOU AND YOUR FUTURE BEST FRIENDS ARE ALL LOOKING AT THE SAME RAINBOW."

GROSS! WHEN DID YOU GET SO CHEESEY?

JUST WRITE IT, SPIKE.

NOT THE END!